for Benjamin

SIMON & SCHUSTER
BOOKS FOR YOUNG READERS
An imprint of Simon & Schuster Children's Publishing Division
1230 Avenue of the Americas, New York, New York 10020
Copyright© 1996 by Lisa Campbell Ernst. All rights reserved including the
right of reproduction in whole or in part in any form. SIMON & SCHUSTER
BOOKS FOR YOUNG READERS is a trademark of Simon & Schuster. Book design
by Lisa Campbell Ernst. The text of this book is set in Goudy Old Style. The
illustrations are rendered in pastel, ink, and pencil. Printed and bound in
Singapore.   10 9 8 7 6 5 4 3 2 1
    Library of Congress Cataloging-in-Publication Data
Ernst, Lisa Campbell. Duke, the Dairy Delight Dog / Lisa Campbell Ernst.—1st ed.
p. cm. Summary: Darla doesn't want a dirty dog around her Dairy Delight, but
Duke patiently tries every tactic to convince her that her shop is his home.
ISBN 0-689-80750-3 (hc) [l. Dogs—Fiction. 2. Home—Fiction.] I. Title.
PZ7.E7323Du 1996 [E]—dc20 95-44057

Duke the Dairy Delight Dog

Lisa Campbell Ernst

Simon & Schuster
Books for Young Readers

For all his long life,
Duke had been a traveling dog.
Year after year he wandered alone from town to town, down back roads and country lanes. He slept beneath the stars at night and ate scraps of food rummaged from trash cans along the way.

Now Duke was so old that his once-brown hair had turned silver on top. Still, Duke thought his life on the road was a good one.

But the morning Duke wandered into Glendale and spied Darla's Dairy Delight, *Home of the Famous Vanilla-Chocolate Swirl*, his life changed forever.

One look at that giant ice cream cone sign, and it was love at first sight—Duke went ga-ga. He imagined the cool ice cream on his tongue and he was giddy, his knees felt like marshmallows. He was a dog agog.

Running to peek in the windows of the tiny, red building, Duke discovered a glimmering ice cream machine that bedazzled him more than the most brilliant galaxy of stars.

And suddenly, Duke knew he would stay forever. "After all these many years and many places," he thought, "I have found my *home*."

With that, Duke sat down.

Now even though Duke knew he was home, what he did not know about was Darla. Darla Snavely, *the* Darla of Darla's Dairy Delight. The Dairy Delight was Darla's pride and joy, and she kept it so clean you could eat off the floor.

So when Darla showed up for work in her crisp Dairy Delight uniform and found a dirty, smelly mass of a dog waiting for her, she let out a shriek.

"Shoo!" Darla screeched, waving her Aztec Pink fingernails at Duke. "Scat, honey lamb! You go on home, now!"

Duke, of course, did not budge. He let out a thunderous "Woof!" which meant, "I *am* home!"

Darla screamed again, ran inside the Dairy Delight and locked the door.

"What the doo-daw!" Darla gasped, pinning her shaken Dairy Delight cap back in place.

By this time Earl, the town sheriff, and Patty from the diner had heard the commotion, and they ran over.

"Problem, Darla?" Earl asked.

"That—that—monster won't leave!" Darla shouted out the little sliding window.

Earl and Patty looked at Duke, who was wagging his tail. "Seems pretty harmless to me," Earl said.

"He's kind of cute," Patty agreed, scratching Duke behind the ears.

"Don't touch that filthy animal!" Darla cried, "You'll only encourage him to stay!" and she slammed the little window closed.

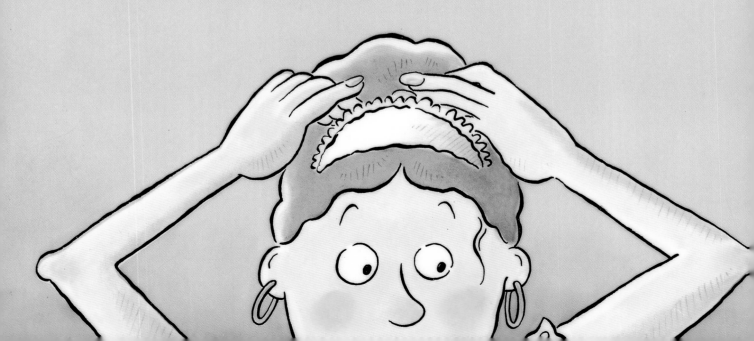

But Duke needed no encouragement. He was staying,
and nothing Darla could say or do would change his mind.
Duke simply sat and waited—thinking of ice cream,
morning, noon, and night.

Over the next few days news spread through town that
Darla had company. Friendly folks from all around brought
Duke food to eat. Some even offered to take him home.
But Duke just wagged his tail, and gazed lovingly at
the Dairy Delight. It was obvious he thought he *was* home.

Of course the more Darla watched Duke sit in front of her beloved Dairy Delight making goo-goo eyes at each ice cream cone that left, the more frazzled she became. "Mangy flea-bag!" she cried, and then threw herself into a cleaning frenzy, trying to stay calm.

Still, Darla was in a royal snit. "Don't drip on the counter!" she snapped at her customers as she served the Dairy Delight's famous Vanilla-Chocolate swirls. "And keep away from that ratty dog!"

Darla scrubbed and buffed and polished like there was no tomorrow.

Days passed slowly for Duke as he sat watching Darla and the Dairy Delight from the outside, but his heart remained steadfast.

It was clear that everyone else in town *except* Darla was quite fond of Duke. "She just needs to get to know me," Duke decided. "But how? If she won't come to me, I'll just have to go to her."

Taking a deep breath, Duke marched right up to the door of the Dairy Delight and stepped in with the next customer.

The whoops and
hollers that burst from Darla's
mouth sent everyone in Glendale
running. The customers inside the Dairy
Delight high-tailed it out, and everyone
else came lickety-split to see what was wrong.
"OUT, OUT, *OUT!*" Darla screamed, running
toward Duke with one of her industrial brooms.
Poor Duke ran faster than he had since he was a pup.
"Crazy mutt!" Darla shrieked.

Outside, Duke was surrounded by townsfolk. "Never
you mind," Patty said. "She's just a persnickety old bat."
And the rest of the crowd agreed.

Darla glared out her window, and set about
sterilizing the Dairy Delight.

But Duke was not so easily discouraged. "She'll come around," he insisted. "She just needs to spend some time with me."

That night Duke examined the little red building from top to bottom.

There was only one way into the Dairy Delight: the front door. "The first time Darla *saw* me come in," Duke thought. "This time I'll just have to sneak in while she's not looking."

And the next day, when Darla turned her back to wipe off a counter, Duke did just that.

Instantly, Darla's keen ears
heard the *click click click* of Duke's
dirty-dog toenails and she ended the
daring attempt with more whoops and hollers.

"Come on, Darla," Earl pleaded, "give
the guy a break! It's obvious he just plain
loves your Dairy Delight. He's not going to
hurt anything."

Duke wagged his tail until Darla
screamed again. "If that filthy canine thinks
he can just waltz in here and call the Dairy
Delight home he's got another thing coming!"

Darla shooed everyone out, turned the sign to
"Closed," and spent the rest of the day cleaning.

Darla had, by now, become such a crab that her customers began to dwindle. "This is all that no-good mongrel's fault," she hissed, scrubbing the ceiling with disinfectant.

Outside, Duke sat planning his next attempt. "So if she *saw* me and she *heard* me," he mused, "I'll just have to sneak in when she can do neither."

Sure enough, the next time Darla turned to fill one of her famous Vanilla-Chocolate swirl cones and the ice cream machine began to rumble and rattle, Duke tip-toed in yet again.

Alas, this time Darla *smelled* the odoriferous Duke, and with one screech and a charge with her favorite mop, Duke was out the door a third time.

Customers were now few and far between. Delivery men came by with new cleaning supplies, but only the bravest of ice cream lovers would weather Darla's fury.

Even Duke began to worry. Still, though, he knew he *must* get through that door. Somehow Darla would grow to like him. He just knew it.

And so Duke sat and waited.

Day after day passed.

Then one morning, a huge box arrived at the Dairy Delight's door. Darla's eyes shone as she unpacked the *Kleen-Rite 3-in-1 Scrubber-Buffer-Waxer* machine. "The ultimate cleaning machine," Darla whispered, touching its huge round scrubbing-buffing-waxing brushes.

Duke peeked gingerly through the window as Darla poured a big, pink pool of peppermint soap on the floor, and turned the monstrous machine on.

Darla's eyes studied the floor. The scrubbing machine roared. The sweet aroma of peppermint filled the air.

And at that very second, Duke saw his last chance.

With one huge lunge Duke was through the door and into the Dairy Delight.

But he had entered with such force that when his right front paw hit the edge of the peppermint soap pool, he shot across the floor, straight into the roaring cleaning machine.

"No, *don't!*" Duke heard Darla scream.

And then everything was a blur of swirling, bumping, and thumping. The machine went crazy as Darla wrestled frantically to control it. Fur mixed with the spinning brushes. Soap bubbles shot in the air, and Darla screamed again.

By the time the townspeople had rushed to the Dairy Delight and Earl finally pulled the plug on the monster machine, it had done its work.

Darla staggered to her feet, and saw the shocked looks on everyone's faces. "I tried to stop it," she cried. "I never meant to hurt him!"

"Look!" she heard someone whisper. "Look at that, it's a Dairy Delight dog."

Darla turned to look. There, standing in front of her was a *Chocolate-Vanilla Swirl*, wagging its tail.

Duke's days at the Dairy Delight had officially begun. He quickly became *the* Dairy Delight dog, and people came from miles around to see his spectacular hairdo, and eat Darla's tasty Vanilla-Chocolate swirls.

Duke paraded his swirls proudly. It seemed to prove to everyone, even Darla, that he really *did* belong at the Dairy Delight. Just like he knew he did. And with time, even Darla grew fond of Duke. Just like he knew she would.

Because, at long last, Darla's Dairy Delight truly *was* *"Home of the Famous Vanilla-Chocolate Swirl."*